THE WIZARD OF OZ

BONNEY PRESS

Published by Bonney Press,
an imprint of Hinkler Books Pty Ltd
45–55 Fairchild Street
Heatherton Victoria 3202 Australia
www.hinkler.com

BONNEY
PRESS

Cover design: Jess Matthews
Illustrator: Geraldine Rodriguez
Text adapted by: Katie Hewat
Design: Paul Scott and Patricia Hodges
Editorial: Emily Murray
Prepress: Splitting Image

ISBN: 978 1 4889 1298 6

Printed and bound in China

THE WIZARD OF OZ

Based on the original story by

L. FRANK BAUM

Dorothy was worried. She stood at the front door and looked out across the dusty grey Kansas prairie. A great wind howled, coming ever closer. The shutters rattled and the little wooden house groaned around her.

Dorothy lived with Uncle Henry and Aunt Em, who were both out working in the fields, nowhere to be seen. Dorothy's little grey dog Toto began to whine, so she picked him up and held him in her arms.

As the great wind raced towards her, it whipped up a dust storm. The house shook and shuddered. Within seconds, the house had filled with wind and then Dorothy felt it lift off the ground and whirl up into the sky!

The little house spun through the air for what seemed like hours, until eventually Dorothy felt it falling. It hit the ground with a great thud. Holding Toto in her arms, Dorothy slowly walked outside. She was shocked at what she saw!

The house had landed in a strange and beautiful land, unlike anywhere Dorothy had ever seen. It was so very bright and beautiful! Tall trees groaned under the weight of ripe fruit and nearby a babbling brook ran past, its banks covered with colourful flowers.

Coming towards her was a group of small, odd-looking people. A much older lady in a stunning sparkly dress was with them. 'I'm the Good Witch of the North. Welcome to the Land of Oz!' she said. She gestured to her companions. 'My friends, the Munchkins, are very grateful to you for killing the Wicked Witch of the East. You have set them free at last.'

Puzzled, Dorothy looked down and saw two legs wearing a pair of sparkly red shoes poking out from underneath her house. She gave a little scream and watched in horror as the legs shrivelled away to nothing, leaving only the shoes.

'Who was she?' Dorothy asked the Good Witch.

'She was a very powerful, wicked witch,' the Good Witch replied, taking in Dorothy's plaited pigtails and blue-and-white-checked dress. 'You must be a great sorceress indeed, even if you do dress rather oddly.' She noticed Dorothy's simple black shoes and gasped as if in pain. 'Ugh! How hideous!' she said, and picked up the Wicked Witch's red slippers. 'You'd better take these. They hold some kind of magical charm or other, but we don't know what it is.'

Dorothy was surprised to find that the lovely slippers fit her perfectly. Thanking the Good Witch, she politely asked for directions back to Kansas, as she knew Aunt Em and Uncle Henry would be terribly worried about her.

'I've never heard of Kansas,' said the Good Witch. 'The Land of Oz is surrounded by a desert. It is impossible to leave.'

Dorothy felt very sad and began to cry softly. Seeing this, many of the Munchkins pulled out their handkerchiefs and began to cry too. They sobbed giant wet tears and blew their noses with noisy honking sounds, which so amused Dorothy that she soon forgot her own tears.

'There is one thing you could try,' said the Good Witch. 'A powerful wizard lives in the Emerald City. He may know a way of getting you home.'

'How can I find the Emerald City?' asked Dorothy.

'You must follow the yellow brick road to the centre of Oz,' she replied. 'But beware! Don't stray from the road.'

Dorothy was determined to find the wizard and get home as soon as possible. She thanked the Good Witch and the Munchkins and set off along the yellow brick road with Toto trotting along beside her.

After several miles, the yellow brick road passed through a cornfield. Beside the road was a scarecrow. As Dorothy and Toto passed by, he winked at them! Dorothy gasped and jumped back, and Toto got such a fright that he leaped into a prickly bush.

'You wouldn't mind lifting me down, would you?' the Scarecrow asked politely. 'I don't weigh much.'

Toto barked and growled at the Scarecrow as he plucked prickles out of his rump with his teeth, but Dorothy thought he seemed nice enough. He was certainly the nicest scarecrow she'd ever met.

Dorothy helped the Scarecrow down to the ground. He thanked her and asked where she was going. Dorothy explained that she was going to see the wizard.

The Scarecrow looked very excited. 'May I come with you?' he asked. 'Maybe the wizard could give me a brain.' He lifted his hat and pulled a handful of straw from his head. 'I so wish to be smart, but I only have straw for brains.'

Dorothy was happy to have company and told the Scarecrow he may join her, and they set off along the yellow brick road together, chatting merrily.

Later that day, they came upon a woodcutter's cottage. Outside it stood a man completely made of tin who was holding an axe in mid-air, ready to chop at a tree branch. He seemed to be frozen in place.

'Would you be so kind as to oil my joints?' the Tin Man asked through his creaky, rusted jaw. Dorothy found an oilcan close by and oiled the Tin Man's joints until he could move freely. He was very grateful.

When Dorothy told the Tin Man where she was going, he asked if he could join them. 'I've heard of the Great Wizard of Oz,' he said, 'and I'm sure he could give me a heart. I only want to love and be loved, but that's very hard without a heart.' He banged on his tin chest with his tin fist, and it made a hollow, clanging sound.

Dorothy agreed that he should join them, and they set off along the yellow brick road once more.

The road led them through a dark and gloomy forest full of strange screeches and squawks and grunts and growls. Suddenly, a huge lion leaped out onto the road ahead of them and let out a ferocious roar. Toto barked and the Lion bared his teeth and tried to bite him!

'Don't you dare eat my dog!' Dorothy cried, stepping forwards and smacking the Lion on the nose. 'You should be ashamed of yourself, a big beast like you, trying to eat a little dog! You are just a big coward!'

The Lion's jaws snapped shut, his eyes welled up, and, to Dorothy's great surprise, he began to cry. 'I've always been a coward,' he said through his sobs. 'I wish I was brave, but I just can't help being scared.'

Dorothy felt very sorry for the poor creature and suggested that he join them on their journey. 'I'm sure the wizard can give you some courage,' she said. The overjoyed Lion promised he would not try to bite Toto again.

They travelled further into the forest and came to a wide river that had a rickety wooden bridge over it. Just as they were about to cross, the group heard terrifying sounds coming from the forest around them.

The Lion gasped in fright. 'The Kalidahs!' he whispered. Several beasts stepped out of the trees and Dorothy saw what had terrified the Lion so. The Kalidahs were giant creatures with bodies like bears and heads like tigers. They had razor-sharp claws and long pointy fangs.

'Everyone get across the bridge!' yelled the Scarecrow.

'We'll never make it!' cried Dorothy.

'I'll hold them off,' said the Lion and he turned to face the Kalidahs. He roared his most terrifying roar, stopping the startled Kalidahs in their tracks. When everyone had reached the far side of the river, the Lion sprang on to the bridge and ran as fast as he could.

The Kalidahs gave chase. The Lion reached the far side as they started to cross, and the Tin Man began to chop at the bridge. The Kalidahs were almost across as the Tin Man struck his final stroke. The bridge gave way with a huge crack and fell into the river and washed some of the Kalidahs away.

Dorothy and her friends hugged each other with relief. Keen to get out of the dark forest, they had a short rest, then continued on their way.

The next morning, they reached the edge of the forest and were very excited to see a shining city in the distance. 'That must be the Emerald City!' cried Dorothy, and she began to run along the road, the others close behind.

As they ran, Dorothy and her friends came upon a vast field of brilliant red flowers. Instead of following the road, which ran in a circle around the field, they took a shortcut through it. They plunged into the field, whooping and leaping and giggling as the flowers tickled their legs.

Little did they know that the flowers possessed a powerful magic. Dorothy soon slowed to a walk. A wave of weariness washed over her and she sat down. Within a few moments, she was fast asleep. Toto, too, slipped into a weary slumber, then the Lion suddenly stopped and dropped to the ground, fast asleep too.

The Scarecrow and the Tin Man were not made of flesh and blood, so they weren't affected by the magic. 'Oh no!' the Scarecrow cried over the Lion's ear-splitting snores. 'We must get them out!'

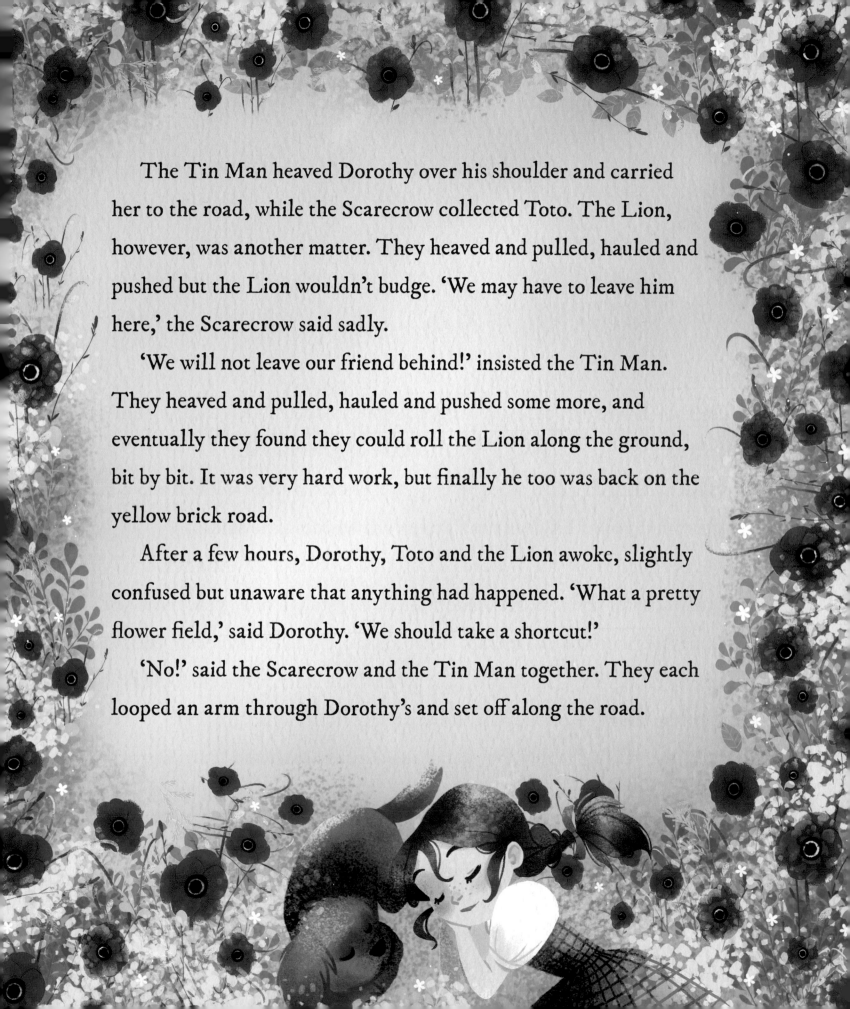

The Tin Man heaved Dorothy over his shoulder and carried her to the road, while the Scarecrow collected Toto. The Lion, however, was another matter. They heaved and pulled, hauled and pushed but the Lion wouldn't budge. 'We may have to leave him here,' the Scarecrow said sadly.

'We will not leave our friend behind!' insisted the Tin Man. They heaved and pulled, hauled and pushed some more, and eventually they found they could roll the Lion along the ground, bit by bit. It was very hard work, but finally he too was back on the yellow brick road.

After a few hours, Dorothy, Toto and the Lion awoke, slightly confused but unaware that anything had happened. 'What a pretty flower field,' said Dorothy. 'We should take a shortcut!'

'No!' said the Scarecrow and the Tin Man together. They each looped an arm through Dorothy's and set off along the road.

Eventually they reached a huge green gate studded with glittering emeralds and surrounded by towering city walls made of green brick.

Dorothy banged three times on the gate. Soon a shutter opened and a man in a green hat poked his head out. 'State your business,' he said.

'We are here to see the Wizard of Oz,' said Dorothy. The man opened the gate and escorted them to the palace. They were taken to a great room with a green marble floor and an emerald-coloured curtain that covered an entire wall.

After waiting for what seemed like a very long time, a voice boomed through the room. 'I am Oz, the Great and Terrible. Who are you?'

Dorothy was frightened, but found the courage to speak. 'I am Dorothy, sir,' she said. 'A great wind carried me and my house to the land of Oz and now I am stranded here.'

'Aha!' boomed the voice. 'So you are the one who killed the Wicked Witch of the East?'

'I suppose I am,' replied Dorothy, 'but it really was an accident.'

'And what do you want of me?' asked the voice.

Dorothy explained that she wished him to help her get home to Kansas. Then she introduced her friends and explained that they sought a brain, a heart and some courage.

After a long pause, the voice replied, 'I will grant all you ask, but first you must complete a task. You must travel to the castle of the Wicked Witch of the West and destroy her.'

Dorothy burst into tears. 'But I've never killed anyone or anything on purpose in my life. And even if I wanted to kill her, I don't have a spare house!'

'You'll think of something. Now go!' boomed the wizard.

The band of friends left the Emerald City and followed the yellow brick road to the strangely empty and quiet lands of the Wicked Witch of the West. They had no idea how they would destroy the Witch, or even if they would be able to find her.

They needn't have worried, however, as the Witch had already seen them from the tallest tower in her castle. Furious that they were trespassing on her land, she hopped up and down, muttering to herself and scratching at her warty face.

Then she took out a golden whistle and blew three long notes. Soon there was a great fluttering and an army of winged monkeys swarmed around her.

'Fetch me that wretched girl and the lion!' the Witch told the King of the Monkeys. 'Destroy the others.'

The winged monkeys nodded and flew away. They grabbed up the Lion and Dorothy, who clutched Toto close to her chest. Then they pulled the stuffing out of the Scarecrow so he was nothing more than a pile of rags and dropped the Tin Man from a great height so that he broke into pieces.

Dorothy and the Lion returned to the forest to find their friends. They put the Tin Man back together and filled the Scarecrow with fresh straw. They were as good as new in no time at all.

The merry little band followed the road back to the Emerald City. The countryside, which had seemed eerie and deserted before, was now filled with people who were all rejoicing the death of the Wicked Witch of the West.

When they arrived back in the Emerald City, they were taken once again to the great room. After a long wait, the voice boomed out, 'You have destroyed the Wicked Witch of the West!'

'Yes,' replied Dorothy. 'Now all we ask is that you give us the rewards you promised.'

'Well,' said the voice, 'that may be somewhat difficult.' As the voice spoke, Toto ran over to the curtain covering the back wall and began tugging at the corner. Soon the whole curtain fell away, and behind it was a little man with thick spectacles, which made his eyes appear very large.

Dorothy was shocked. 'Why, you're not a wizard! You're just a man!' she exclaimed.

The man huffed and puffed as if about to argue, but finally came further into the room. 'I'm sorry, dear,' he sighed. 'I arrived in Oz when my hot air balloon drifted away from my homeland and landed here. The people thought I was a wizard, as I came from the sky. I was a little frightened, so I let them believe it.'

'But why did you promise us help you couldn't give?' asked Dorothy, feeling very sad.

'I meant well,' replied Oz. 'I have grown to care for the people of this land very much. You did us all a great service by ridding us of the Wicked Witch.'

'But what about my brain?' asked the Scarecrow.

'And my heart?' asked the Tin Man.

'And my courage?' asked the Lion.

Oz jumped up from his chair excitedly. 'I believe I can help with those,' he said and he ran off behind the curtain.

When Oz returned, he lifted off the Scarecrow's hat and filled his head with a handful of pins and needles. Then he sewed it up. 'From now on, you shall certainly be sharp-witted!' said Oz.

The Scarecrow was delighted. 'I feel so smart!' he said. 'I'd tell you all the smart things I'm thinking, but only I'm clever enough to understand.' Dorothy smiled.

She thought the Scarecrow had been perfectly smart all along.

Oz went behind the curtain again and this time returned with a small satin heart filled with sawdust. He cut a small hole in the Tin Man's chest, placed in the heart and repaired the hole. 'Now you have a brand-new heart!' he said.

The Tin Man was overjoyed. He hugged everyone in the room and told them he loved them so very much. Dorothy giggled, thinking how kind-hearted the Tin Man had been since the day she met him.

Finally, Oz went behind the curtain and returned with a bottle of liquid, which he offered to the Lion. 'Drink this and you'll be the bravest Lion in Oz,' he said.

The Lion gulped down the liquid quickly, then pranced and prowled around the room, bellowing his most ferocious roar ever. Oz leaned over and winked at Dorothy. 'It was only water in the bottle, but it seems to have helped him find his inner courage,' he whispered. This made Dorothy giggle again. After their very first meeting, she'd always found the Lion to be very courageous indeed.

'Now, my dear,' Oz said to Dorothy, 'I have an idea that might just see us both home. We'll make another hot air balloon and sail across the desert all the way to Kansas. My home is not far from there.'

Over the next days and weeks, Oz, Dorothy and her friends worked on the balloon until it was finally ready. Oz and Dorothy said a tearful goodbye to their friends and the townsfolk, then climbed into the basket. The balloon began to rise, but at the last moment, Toto leaped out of Dorothy's arms and ran off. Dorothy immediately jumped out to chase him.

The balloon lifted from the ground and began to strain against the ropes that held it down. 'Hurry, my dear!' cried Oz. But finally – snap! – the ropes broke, and the balloon sailed away.

'Farewell!' cried Oz, waving as the balloon rose higher and higher. That was the last anyone ever heard of the Great Wizard of Oz, but he was always remembered fondly.

Poor Dorothy slumped to the floor and began to cry. She cried and cried until she heard a soft, friendly voice say, 'No need for tears.'

Dorothy looked up to see a kindly looking lady with rich red hair and bright blue eyes, wearing a beautiful white dress. 'I am Glinda, the Good Witch of the South.'

'Pleased to meet you,' said Dorothy, hiccupping as she tried to control her sobs. 'But you don't understand ... now I will never get home.'

'Oh, yes you will,' said Glinda cheerfully. 'Your shoes contain a very special type of magic. Just knock your heels together three times and ask to be carried to wherever you would like to go.'

If she had known, Dorothy could have gone home any time she liked! But then she would never have had such a grand adventure and made so many wonderful friends.

Dorothy smiled and dried her tears. She hugged each of her friends tightly, then picked up Toto and tapped her heels together three times. 'Home to Kansas!' she said.

Instantly, she and Toto went whirring through the air, so swiftly that all Dorothy could feel was the wind whistling past her ears. In no time at all, she felt a gentle bump as she landed on the ground again.

'Good gracious!' Dorothy cried as she looked around. She was back home at the little farm on the prairie. There was even a new house in place of the one the wind had blown away.

And there was Aunt Em rushing towards her. 'Darling girl, wherever did you come from?' she asked as she folded Dorothy into her arms and covered her face with kisses.

'From the Land of Oz,' said Dorothy gravely. 'And I'm so glad to be at home again!'